Baby Bear comes home

Antony Lishak · Illustrated by Ian Newsham

BLue Bananas

For the real Jessica

Baby Bear comes home

Antony Lishak · Illustrated by Ian Newsham

MAMMOTH

First published in Great Britain 1996
by W H Books Ltd and Mammoth, imprints of Reed International Books Ltd
Michelin House, 81 Fulham Road, London SW3 6RB
and Auckland, Melbourne, Singapore and Toronto
10 9 8 7
Text copyright © Antony Lishak 1996
Illustrations copyright © Ian Newsham 1996
The author has asserted his moral rights
The illustrator has asserted his moral rights
Paperback ISBN 0 7497 1828 5
Hardback ISBN 0 434 97461 7
A CIP catalogue record for this title
is available from the British Library
Produced by Mandarin Offset Ltd
Printed at Oriental Press, Dubai, U.A.E.

Jessica was tired after

her first day at school.

After tea she went straight to bed.

Jessica dreamt of all the exciting things that had happened to her during the day.

She didn't hear her two bears talking.

Jessica had left Baby Bear at school.

Mother and Father Bear had to go
and find him.

The two bears tiptoed to the top of the
stairs and peeped over the edge.

Step by step the bears climbed down the

stairs. Father Bear held his breath and

kept his eyes shut tight.

Mother Bear led the way to the kitchen.

Mother Bear tiptoed gingerly.

Basher, the cat, was in the way.

He was taking a catnap.

He looked like a monster to Father Bear.

The bears were both nervous.

Mother Bear had seen Basher catch a

mouse and toss it in the air like a ball!

But she didn't tell Father Bear.

13

Basher's sleepy purr rumbled on.

Slowly the bears edged past him

and got to the cat flap.

They pushed it hard and

tumbled out onto the step.

They ran to the garden gate and

out into the street.

The path was wet after the rain.

The silver face of the moon quivered

like a jelly in the puddles.

I'm not sure.

Father Bear was cold. He began to
jog along the pavement to keep warm.
Then something dreadful happened.
'Whoosh' – he slipped right off the
pavement and into the road!

Father Bear tried to hold on to the kerb.

But a river of rainwater carried

him along the gutter.

Mother Bear picked up a branch that

had blown down from a tree.

She held it out for Father Bear to grab.

She was too late!

Father Bear missed the branch

and floated towards the drain.

Luckily he was stopped by a pile

of leaves. Poor old Father Bear was

like a soggy sponge.

In the dark, everything looked so strange.

The bears were lost.

Just then, an owl landed in the tree above their heads. 'I can see the school from here,' he said. 'Follow me.'

Owl flapped his wings and flew off into the night.

The bears followed the owl into the park
until they came to a pond. Owl swooped
down over the water and flew off into
the darkness.

But the bears were left behind.

They could not fly like Owl.

Mother Bear found an empty bottle.
She put it on the pond and sat on it
carefully. Father Bear held tight to Mother
Bear and they paddled across the pond.

But the bottle had no top and water flowed into it. The bears paddled harder, but the bottle filled up faster. It tossed and swayed like a ship in a storm...

Then the bottle sank.

The two wet bears pulled

themselves onto a large lily leaf.

They were startled by a croak

from the water. There was a splash,

and two frogs leapt out of the pond.

The frogs told the bears to

climb on their backs.

They held on tight as the frogs

skimmed the water.

At the edge of the pond they said

farewell to the frogs.

Owl was waiting for them at the school.

The bears raced to the school, heading straight for the front door.

Baby Bear heard the flap of the letterbox
and rushed out into the corridor.
The three bears were together at last.

40

Before they set off, Baby Bear took

them to meet his new friends.

41

Then the three bears held paws and ran down the corridor.

They squeezed through the letterbox and out into the dark night.

But there was one last surprise!

Basher was there, waiting.

He had been following them all along.

There was a flurry of feathers.

Owl had come to the rescue.

Basher pounced and swiped a claw
at Owl. But he was too late. Owl took off
safely with the bears on his back.

Owl soared high over the town.

The bears held on tightly and looked

for Jessica's house.

Soon the bears were snuggled up beside
Jessica. Mother and Father Bear went to
sleep at once, but Baby Bear was wide
awake. He was looking forward to playing
hide and seek again tomorrow.